Suggestions for Parents

First, read the book to your child. Allow him or her all the time needed to look closely at the pictures and to discuss the story. Then—even on another day—read the story again, now pointing to the words as you read them. After a few readings, the child who is ready to read will begin to pick up the often-repeated words—even the big ones! Before long (there's no hurry) the child will try to read the book alone. It is most important that you patiently build your child's confidence and give him or her the sense that reading is fun. You will find that there is nothing to match the excitement and satisfaction your child will feel on learning to read *a whole book*!

The Marvelous Mud Washing Machine

By Patty Wolcott

Illustrated by Richard Brown

Random House 🏠 New York

Library of Congress Cataloging-in-Publication Data
Wolcott, Patty.
   The marvelous mud washing machine / by Patty Wolcott ;
illustrated by Richard Brown.
       p.   cm. — (Ten-word readers)
   Originally published: Reading, Mass. : Addison-Wesley, 1974.
   Summary: A young boy with an affinity for mud
also has a unique way of washing for dinner.
   ISBN 0-679-81926-6 (trade) — ISBN 0-679-91926-0 (lib. bdg.)
   [1. Mud—Fiction.   2. Cleanliness—Fiction.]   I. Brown, Richard
Eric, 1946–ill.   II. Title.   III. Series: Wolcott, Patty. Ten-word readers.
PZ7.W8185Mar   1991
[E]—dc20   91-8196

Manufactured in the United States of America
10 9 8 7 6 5 4 3 2 1

Beautiful marvelous mud.
Marvelous beautiful mud.

Beautiful marvelous
marvelous marvelous!
Beautiful marvelous mud!

Wash for dinner now.
Wash for dinner now.
Dinner! Dinner!
Wash for dinner.
Wash for dinner now.

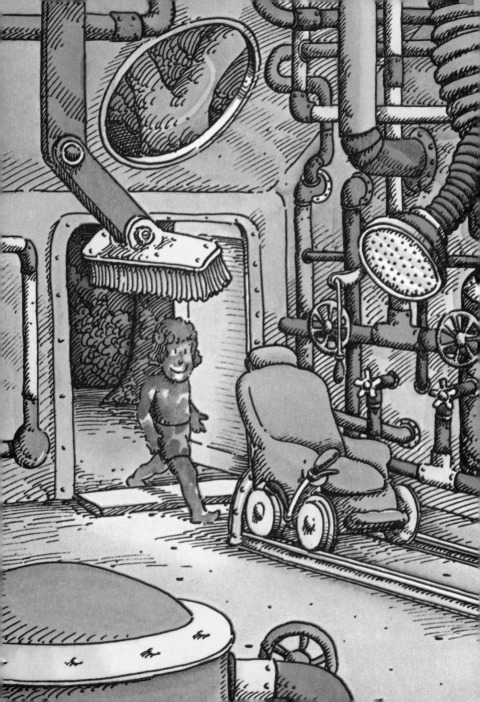

Washing machine, now wash!
Washing machine, now wash!
Washing machine,
washing machine,
washing machine, now wash!

Washing, washing, washing, wash.

Washing, washing,
washing, wash.

Wash, wash, wash, wash,
wash, wash, wash.

Washing machine,
wash, wash.

Beautiful marvelous washing machine,

washing machine,
washing machine.

Marvelous beautiful washing machine.

Marvelous
beautiful wash!

Beautiful marvelous boy!
Marvelous beautiful boy!
Marvelous marvelous
marvelous marvelous!
Beautiful marvelous boy!